Pinkalicious

and Aqua, the Mini-Mermaid

HARPER FESTIVAL

An Imprint of HarperCollinsPublishers

by Victoria Kann

To Antonia
—V.K.

The author gratefully acknowledges the
artistic and editorial contributions of
Daniel Griffo and Natalie Engel.

HarperFestival is an imprint of HarperCollins Publishers.

Pinkalicious and Aqua, the Mini-Mermaid
Copyright © 2016 by Victoria Kann

Based on the HarperCollins book *Pinkalicious* written by
Victoria Kann and Elizabeth Kann, illustrated by Victoria Kann
For information address HarperCollins Children's Books,
a division of HarperCollins Publishers, 195 Broadway, New York, NY 10007.
www.harpercollinschildrens.com

Library of Congress Control Number: 2015938896
ISBN 978-0-06-241075-7

Book design by Kirsten Berger
19 20   CWM   20 19 18 17 16 15 14 13 12
❖
First Edition

Peter and I were going to see our merminnie friend, Aqua, for a special playdate! She was going to show us all her favorite seaside spots.

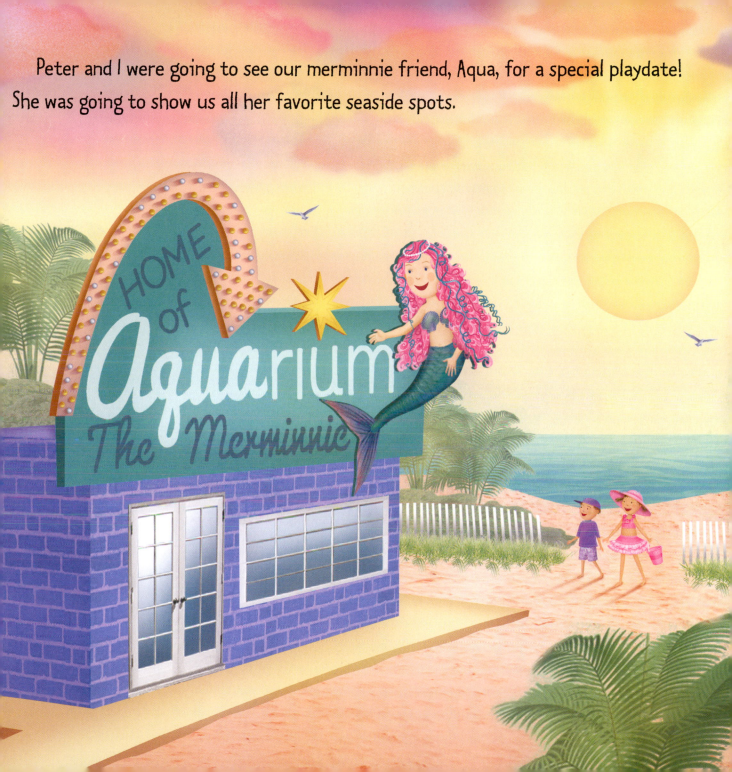

We headed over to the aquarium, where Aqua lives. When we arrived, we found Aqua in a tank full of colorful creatures.

"Hi, Aqua," I said. "Ready to go?"

"Just a moment," she replied. "I'm almost done teaching this school of fish how to mambo."

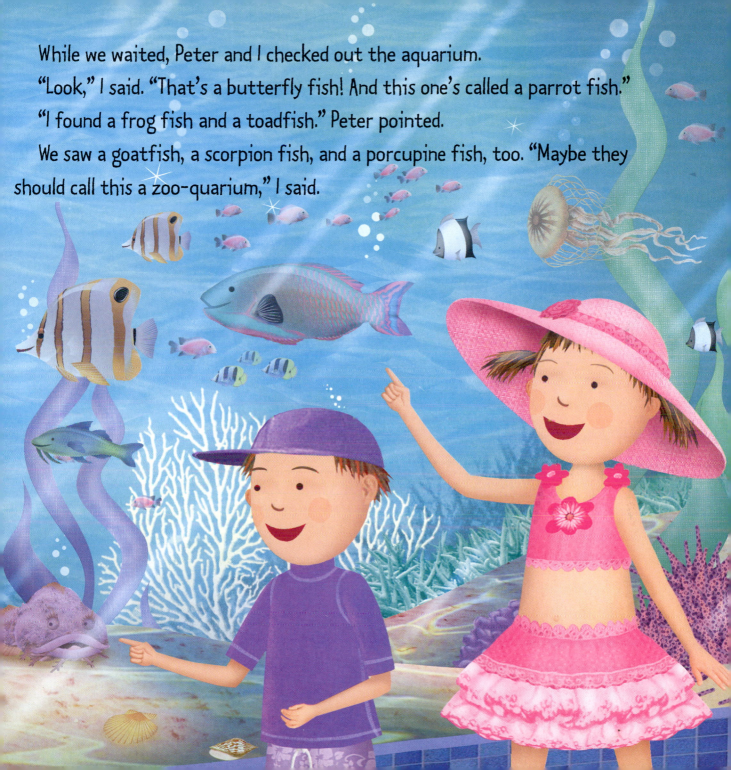

While we waited, Peter and I checked out the aquarium.

"Look," I said. "That's a butterfly fish! And this one's called a parrot fish."

"I found a frog fish and a toadfish." Peter pointed.

We saw a goatfish, a scorpion fish, and a porcupine fish, too. "Maybe they should call this a zoo-quarium," I said.

At last, Aqua was ready for our adventure. She met us outside. "Let's go this way," she said, motioning toward the ocean.

We scooped up Aqua in my pink bucket and skipped through the surf. Soon we reached a big hole filled with water.

"Welcome to the tide pool," said Aqua. We leaned over the edge and peeked in. There were starfish, clams, and sea plants everywhere! It was like a miniature ocean, perfect for our miniature friend.

"This is my favorite spot to think," said Aqua. "Clams make great listeners."

Peter stepped on something flat and smooth as we walked along the coast.

"What's this?" he said.

"Oh," cried Aqua. "A sand dollar! How wonderful!"

Peter's eyes widened. "A sand dollar? Excuse me, Aqua, but I need to borrow this bucket."

Aqua and I relaxed on the shore as Peter hunted for sand dollars. "Should we tell him it's not real money?" Aqua whispered. "Maybe in a minute," I said.

Just then, we heard a big rumble. "Oh, the waves are loud today," Aqua marveled.

"Actually, that was my tummy," I said. "Excuse me." It was definitely time for a snack.

"I know just the place," said Aqua.

Our merminnie guided us to a grove of palm trees with more coconuts than you could count!

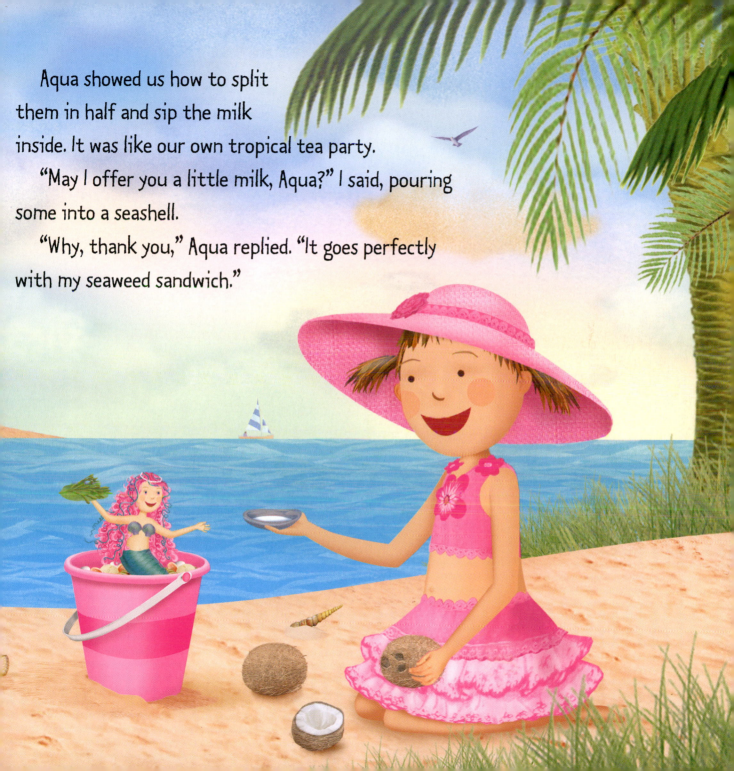

Aqua showed us how to split them in half and sip the milk inside. It was like our own tropical tea party.

"May I offer you a little milk, Aqua?" I said, pouring some into a seashell.

"Why, thank you," Aqua replied. "It goes perfectly with my seaweed sandwich."

After we ate, Aqua said she had one more place to show us. "But this one is a surprise," she said with a smile.

She led us to a cove and told us to close our eyes. We walked very, very slowly. "Now," said Aqua, "look around you."

In the cove was the most beautiful collection of ocean treasure we had ever seen. There were seashells of every shape and color. Pieces of sea glass sparkled in the sunlight.

"This is where I keep all the treasure I find on my sea adventures," said Aqua. "It's my special collection. Do you like it?"

But Peter and I couldn't answer. We were simply speechless.

The three of us sat in the cove and looked out at the ocean. Everything was peaceful and quiet.

Suddenly, Peter stood up. "Uh-oh," he said. "I think we've got company."

Off in the distance, we saw two fins poking out of the water. They were swimming toward us fast.

"Are those sharks?" I asked Aqua.

She gulped. "I hope not," she said.

The fins got closer and closer. I was scared. "What are we going to do?" said Peter.

"Maybe they just want to be friends," I said, though I wasn't so sure there was such a thing as a friendly shark.

Just then, the creatures burst out of the water. They weren't sharks at all. They were dolphins. And not only that—they were *pink* dolphins!

"Of course," said Aqua. "I should have known. Pinkalicious and Peter, meet Sandy and Shelly. They pass through here around this time every year."

"How do you do?" I said, curtsying.

"Thank goodness you aren't sharks!" said Peter.

Sandy and Shelly bobbed their heads and squealed. Then they jumped way up high and did double flips.

"I think they like you," said Aqua. "They're putting on a show!"

Sandy and Shelly leaped and twisted and twirled and splashed. When they were done, they nudged us with their noses.

"They want you to join them," said Aqua.

Peter looked at me. I looked at Peter. A swim with the dolphins? How could we resist?

As the sun began to set, we knew it was time to go home. Sandy and Shelly gave the three of us a ride back to the aquarium.

"Good-bye," we called from the beach as their fins disappeared back into the ocean.

We waved good-bye to Aqua and thanked her for showing us all her favorite spots. "The beach is full of magic," I said, "and you're the most marvelous part."

"Yeah," said Peter. "That's for sure!"

As I lay in bed that night, I could still smell the salty sea air.
I made a wish upon a sea star that I'd be back to visit soon.

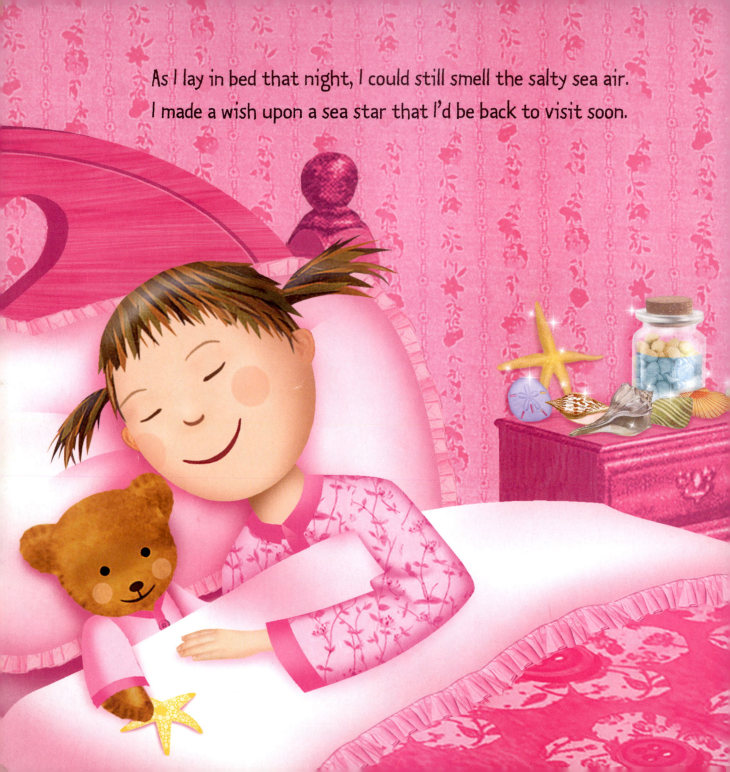